This Story is written by B. E. Wasner.

B. E. WASNER

MEMORIES OF MY LIFE OR LOOKING BACK ON THEM!!

A TRUE STORY.

Impressum

Bibliographic information from the German National Library: The German National Library lists this publication in the Deutsche Nationalbibliografie; detailed bibliographic data can be accessed on the Internet at http://dnb.dnb.de.

© 2023 B. E. WASNER

Herstellung und Verlag: BoD – Books on Demand, Norderstedt

ISBN: 978-3-7568-6198-9

IN MEMORY:

FOR MY MOTHER LUCY WHO LEFT THIS WORLD WAY TO EARLY IN LIFE!

MEMORIES OF MY LIFE OR LOOKING BACK ON THEM!!

FROM 30 MARCH 1953 UNTIL TODAY IN 2023.

They say you should never start a sentence with the letter " I " !! So now I can start writing. I'm a US Army brat as they call us kids. Born on 30. March 1953 in Frankfurt on the river Main, West Germany, Europe, at 8:10 O'clock in the morning.

As I was 6 months old, we moved to the States, on the East Coast. To Connecticut where my dad's older sister and her family lived. My Aunt's name was Edith. I guess that is where I got my middle name from and from my mom's mom whose name was also Edith. My first name I got from my other Grandma Bertha, only I spell my name Berta. My Grandma wanted that she had said this to her son Fritz who was my dad.

We lived on the East Coast until 1958. Somewhere before I was born meaning before 1952, my dad served in the Korean War and was one year long a Prisoner Of War there. The Korean War was between 1950 and 1953. In World War II, my dad was also a Prisoner Of War in Japan one year long. And somewhere between April 1966 and Spring 1968 he also served in the Vietnam War. The same thing also happened here, one year as Prisoner Of War! As he went into retirement in Spring 1968, he was an SP6 E6. Shortly after this, in April 1968 my mom Lucy passed away at age 40. On August 14 of that year, she would have turned 41 years old, R.I.P. Lucy, I will love you forever.

* *

Around fall 1958, I was between 5 ½ and 6 years old, when I got sick. This illness changed all of our lives. At this time my dad was stationed at the Panama Channel Zone. Up to this time I was a " normal girl" who could do anything that other kids could do too: Run, Swim and Jump around, climb Trees and ride a Bike. I could even read and write. I could tell anyone that asked, the exact time it was from the Church clock. Then suddenly 4 other Army kids and I got very sick at the same time. Deadly sick! The illness was something like Polio by much worse because it causes permanent damage of the brain cells. It was Brain Fever!!

I really don't know how long the other kids lived or even if any two of them where even related to each other? Some people say that 2 kids died away shortly after getting sick. The other 2 kids lived a little while longer, being mutable handicapped. And even though I was blind for 7 weeks and totally lame from my neck down to my toes with a breathing tube in my throat; I got through at the best because later I was only handicapped with my body and not handicapped in my mind too. Even though the Doctors did not think that I would make it. That is why they put me into the so called dying room, where I could go in peace. I had been lying in the Hospital for months even getting my eye lights back. But my mom was not ready to let me go, after almost dying herself at my birth. She was praying very hard to God, trusting him. I already saw the light at the end of the tunnel, as the saying is called, I could feel the warm sun at the tunnels end, but then I was pulled back into the dark cold real world being reborn as a 6 year old. But not as the child I once was, but as a 6 year old baby. I could do nothing, not walk, not sit, and not even crawl. My spine cord was as weak as a newborn's is. I had to really learn everything like a newborn. How to hold a spoon and fork, get tied up onto my chair to sit at all. To get pillows all around to sit on the sofa, just learn everything. So you can see that a Mother's love can even be stronger then death sometimes. While the Doctors where fighting to save my life giving me all kinds of meds from all over the World, even experimental ones from a petri dish, a nurse who was a friend of the family said that I looked like an oversized Strawberry! There was no place on my body where they had not set the shots to save me. And no wonder that up to this day I'm scared of shots and needles.

Well somehow, I got along, and in 1959 I got to California over South Carolina on a US Medical plane, lying under an oxygen tent. After being in San Francisco a few months, an Army Doctor told my mom that her 6-year-old girl would never walk again, and it would have been better if she were dead. Well, I'm an Aries born child that has big horns and runs her head against the wall. So, I made a Liar out of this Doctor a few months later as we were at the Hospital for an exam. And I seeing the Doctor walking along the

floor called out to him. I was walking a few pac-
es ahead of my mom freely as he turned
around. He was dumb struck, the look on his
face was priceless, laugh.

He just stood there a moment, then came over
to us and said: "Never again will I Underestimate
the fighting will of a child in this way."

One year later moved 100 miles farther north to
Sonoma County Area right off Highway 101. The
small town located 7 miles south of Santa Rosa
& 7 miles east of Bodega Bay. Anyone who
knows the Movie "The Birds" from Alfred Hitch-
cock knows these 2 Towns and the Region that I
mean.

My Grandma came to live with us in California,
but she also died there in 1960. I was 7 years

old at this time. My brother Kurt was born on October 03, 1960 in San Francisco, California. My parents adopted him 18 months later. December 31, 1962, we moved to Giessen, Germany where my dad was stationed, giving our house for this time up for Rent in California, until we came back in April 1966.

This means second half of 3rd, Grade after the Christmas vacation, over the 4th and the 5th Grade, plus the 6th Grade until April 1966.

* *

Well, it seems I'm doing pretty well, I'm still alive. Just feeling my age and being stuck to an electrical Wheelchair and needing help from a social nurse's station 2 times a day. To help wash me and get me out of bed in the mornings and back into bed later in the day. This way I can stay in my Apt. and do not have to go to a Nursing Home.

* *

My Dad was born a triplet boy on March 31, 1923, in Stolp, Pommern, Germany. (Now it belongs to Poland.)

His name was Fritz, my uncles names were Heinz and Kurt. As the boys where 3 years old in 1925, the family move to the States. They moved to Connecticut. After leaving school, my dad went to the US Coast Guards. His group was also in World War II on a transport Ship. My one uncle was by the Air Force, the other uncle was stationed in a Submarine Unit. This uncle died in World War II. My other uncle died years later. My dad died as the last of the 3 boys on July 04, 2003, at age 80. After he died, I learned that he had Cancer. That's life.

* *

My mom Lucy was born on August 14. 1927 in New York. Because her mom had to work to feed the family, Lucy was raised by her grandma (her Mother's Mom). She was a registered Nurse. Up to this day I only have a picture of her in my heart and in my mind. It is an oil painting of her in her full nurse's uniform. It was always hanging in our hallway.

Just 3 weeks after I turned 15 years old in 1968, Lucy passed away, in the same house as Grandma 8 years before. I still have gotten really over it even after all these years.

We lived in this beautiful house until October 1969 when we moved to Germany forever, selling the house.

* *

In Germany we lived in two apartments belonging to her and her dad. Lilo and dad living in one apartment, Kurt and I together with Grandpa in the other one. Lucy, Lilo and Dad knew each other even before I was born.

On April 20, 1970, Fritz and Lilo got married. Lilo was born on August 18, 1925, in Frankfurt on the river Main, Germany.

I had met Lilo and her parents in the 1960's, but I never met her older sister Annemarie who lived in Canada. Only her older brother Wolfgang who also lived in Canada, on the day we took their father to his grave, on March 30, 1976. Right, it was on my birthday, and I was engaged to Guenther at this time. We got married a few months later.

* *

Guenther was born July 31, 1946, in Biberach on the river Riss. He is the youngest of 5 children.

Guenther and I got married on June 30, 1976. We were together for 7 years then in 1981 we got divorced. I never got married again, just went on living with my animals.

My 2 babies laying down and sleeping.

* *

Sometime after this the Social Ambulant Nurse's Station started to help me.

We moved in 1980 to a different street in the town where I lived for 28 years. I had never lived for so long a time in one place before. Then 9/11, 2009 I moved up the road again, where I still live today. When I moved in 2009, I had my two Maine-Coons, Siamese cats that were born in May 2002. In 2019 at the age of 17 years I had to let my white boy go over the Rainbow Bridge, he had gotten very sick. My two baby boys were born about 2 weeks apart. Their mothers were Sisters, they were the Maine-Coon mix cats. The father was a pure breed Siamese cat. My white cat had beautiful blue/green eyes. Now I have only my Muti-Colored baby that is turning 21 years old in May 2023. We are both getting old, but we are still together and that's what counts.

* *

I have had many Operations also in 2019 when my baby got sick. Too many to write down here. And I was in too many Schools as an Army Brat moving around all the time. Only in Germany was I able to stay in School for a few years as a kid. From the second half of the 3rd grade in 1963 until the 6th grade in April 1966. Back in California I was in Junior High School all 3 years from 7th grade until 9th grade. Then before going back to Germany forever, I was in Senior High School 10th grade for 1 month in 1969. The next time I went back to School it was in Germany in the School year 1970-1971.

* *

We sold our house in California and in October 1969 we flew from San Francisco to Frankfurt on the river Main in Germany, over Los Angeles and New York. We lived in Frankfurt until 1971 where we moved up north of Frankfurt where my parents had built a house in a very small village, with just 21 families and about 100 persons, a small store, a fire department, a post office and a small hotel.

I lived in this village from 1971-1974. In this time, I had to go to the hospital for a few months. I was having issues. That is where I learned the hard way not to trust people. After already being at the US Army Hospital on the Ward for Nerve sickness and getting pumped up with meds that did not come from the Doctor's Order. The Medical Assistant of the Ward just thought he could treat me like a GI Girl, so to keep me quiet as he called it, he gave me 3 times 3 Valium 10/a day = 9 Valium each day before each Meal. One day I did not want to take them, so standing in line like all people from the hospital because everybody that does not have to stay in bed eats in this Cantina. I said: "No, I don't want the meds. That was the first and last time I said this." As if I were a disobeying GI, he pulled my Head back onto my Neck with a yank, put the meds in my mouth and pushed them with his finger down my throat almost making me choke. This made everyone near us gasps, because I was not a GI Girl, but just a civil child barely of age, meaning 21 years old. One of the GI's from my Ward reported shortly after other incidents to the Ward Doctor that I was getting 3 times 3 yellow Valium 10 meds every day from the medic GI. The Doctor was raging!

He was so mad, that he called in other GI's before calling me in, asking if it was true what he had heard? Yes, it is, they said sadly. And this medic Guy was a "Bull" of a Guy. No one can resist him easily. Just the same, after calling me in and talking awhile, getting this guy transferred somewhere else, the Doctor started helping to get me 'Clean'. This time he gave the order to start giving me 3 times a day 2 Valium 10 over one week. Then he would check if he could more away. At this time, I never got tired from the meds like sleepwalking, only being slow in reacting. When I got home from the hospital, I was down to 1 Valium 10 tab. a day. At home my dad gave me the meds before breakfast. Poor dad, because the meds are yellow my dad was trying to make me believe I was taking Vitamin A 1, they are also yellow too. Of course, I knew better but never said anything. I just bravely took them. Then came the day I had to go to a German Nerve Doctor for a checkup. Just like every day I took my meds before breakfast, suddenly my mom's called from the back of the house don't give her the meds today. I just called back, "Too late." The look on my dad's face was priceless! I was due to get a Brain test that day and it was the first time since I was on Valium 10 that I got sleepy. I could hardly keep my eyes opened.

* *

My parents were talking so much that the Doctor who was trying to make the brain test sends both of them out of the room, then he said: "What's Up?" My answer was first Sorry. Then I told him how I had been on 3 times 3 Valium 10 a day without a doctor's order at the US Army

Hospital because of the medical GI that wanted to keep me quiet. Now with the Doctors help over weeks, I'm down to 1 tab. a day in the morning. My dad gives me the meds, today too before my stepmom could stop him. She said don't give her the meds. And I said, too late. But this is the first time that I take them that I'm tired". So, to finish the test, the Doctor called his Assistant, and they taped open my eyes. When everything was done the Doctor just said that we may have to repeat the test in a few weeks, we will just wait and see. He had noted that I had been given 1 Valium 10 tab. that morning before the test.

* *

After a while I went to the German Nerve Hospital on my own will and not by Law. As I was in there, they helped me go to another Hospital, to get an operation on my right leg and hip. This Hospital sends me to an eye doctor to get new eyeglasses and to a dentist to get my teeth fixed. After my Leg and Hip were ok, I was back in the Nerve Hospital.

Yeh, this Head Doctor on whose Ward I was is the reason that I don't trust anyone anymore. One time in a meeting I told him everything that was bothering me, trusting that the doctor would not talk to anyone about it without asking me first. Well as it is Shit happens!!!! And that was the end of me trusting anyone anymore no matter who it was. But most of all not trusting Doctors!

Sometimes it takes me months to trust someone, others I don't even trust after years.

One day this Head Doctor called my parents together for a meeting with me. The Doctor even turned the Lady Doctor who shared this office with him, out of it for the meeting.

She told me as she left the room, if you need me; I'm right down the hall in the Nurse's office. Come if you have too.

Well, there we were the 4 of us. The odds were against me, 3/1. Then the first bomb hit! The Doctor told my parents everything I had told him! With the words changed around a bit. I quess he thought I would not notice that. Then came the next bomb! This time it was my dad saying I had tried to poison my family as a kid with a cake. That my mom had been smoking so much because of me, that she had gotten Lung Cancer and died because of that. Then for the first time at this meeting I shouted "STOP!" You always told me that Lucy had a Heart attack!! Yes, that and Cancer too. You know that quit well he said. But I had not known it. Then he topped it by saying: "If it were not for you, your mother would still be living today. You should have died as a 6-year-old, when you were so sick. Then my dad also said that I had poisoned the pet they had in day care because his owner was on vacation.

Then my Stepmom came up with things that had happened as she said and that I was the one who had done these things.

This was all too much for me. I got off my seat and walked right out of the room not saying one word to anyone, but slamming the office door so hard that all of the windowpanes in the recreation room shook and the doors too. I went to the Nurses office, knocked on the door and broke down in the Lady Doctors arms after the door was opened. All I could say was: "He told them everything they blame me for things too." I was shaking like a leaf, pale as death, my Heart was racing, and I was freezing.

The Doctor asked one nurse please to help her get me to the coach, then get some blankets. She asked the other nurse to please get 2 shots fixed, one to calm me down with my racing Heart and one to help me sleep later if needed and to a pot of Camille tee to also help calm me down. Then she two more wishes, first to leave her alone with me when the Tee and Shots were ready, by switching the phone to the upper Nurse's office and leaving a note that the nurses are upstairs. Closing the drapes over the windows of the office and putting the sign on the door that says: "DO NOT DISTURB!" And second, to try and find a woman who is willing to trade the Wards with me. Someone who goes upstairs so that I can come downstairs to her Ward. She said I need rest now to try and calm down. The Lady Doctor wanted me by all means downstairs on her Ward. Until this time I was on "his" Ward. The Lady Doctor was the only person that I really trusted in the whole Hospital. Well, it did not take so long to find a woman who was willing to trade Wards with me. This Woman had a good friend in the upstairs Ward that she could only visit. By trading with me, they could be together all the time. The trade was made in the afternoon and that I was in the new Ward. The Doctor gave me the first shot and stayed near me until I became quiet, then she put more blankets around me and went to the desk to do some work she had brought with her from the office when she had to leave it. Around supper time I was doing a little better, but still the nurses brought the meal for us in the office.

To help me so that I don't have to go back home, they helped me come to this Job learning center for handicapped people in Isny in Allgaeu.

* *

1974, now I'm at this Job learning center for handicapped people. Not all too far from here, only a few hours is the Bodensee = called in English "Floor Sea". I sounds nutty I know. Its bounders on 3 European countries.

In the first few weeks I made new friends and went through a test program called "Job testing." You could run through many kinds of job testing and training to find out what kind of job works best for you? Is it working with wood, or printing, doing things around Electric stuff and electronics. Railroading or Office stuff. If it had gone my Stepmom's way, I would have gone right to Office learning. She had been an Office worker herself. But the Dean of this place said: "STOP!" Let the girl do the 6-week job testing program, and then she still divides where she wants to go to learn a job. After this 6-week job training, I went to Office learning, because it was I who wanted to learn this way on my own choice and not because my Stepmom wanted me to go there. This job training went on until summer 1975.

* *

Summer 1975, job training is over, I got a finishing record that says I reached 75 from 100% of the points that you can get at the graduation. After moving to town where I live to this day, I started working.

··

I lived in a mother and child caring Home. Being the only Woman there without a child. This was a care taking home for girls' underage mostly. Who already have or are getting a baby and cannot stay at their own home for any reason. Some older Women were also there with the children because gotten beaten up from their mates.

In this home the children where in day care, so that the girls and women can go to school and to work. One of the Women was a nurse in our town hospital. The younger girls can finish school this way or learn a job. Some of them like me also work in rooms belonging to the mother and child home, in a building that belongs to a BMW Automobile shop. I worked there a few years. Then I went to work in a Workshop for handicapped people for a few years. After that I was jobless and looking for work for more than 11 years. Then around 1989 I went back to the Workshop for handicapped people, this time in my hometown until September 1996. That was the Year that I got my handicapped pension. Later that month I went to Daycare from Monday-Friday.

In September 2009 I went back to the Workshop for handicapped people for test working. After moving one more time from one housing area to another housing area in my town. Sometime after this I went back to the Workshop for good until I reached my Pension age of 65 years.

All this time I was in a Program called "Home Caring". You can live in your own home (apartment) and get help from a social care worker who comes to you at home and helps out where 'he' or 'she' can. My last social care worker was together with me over 25 years. He still helps me out where he can. We are very good friends.

****

Then I was jobless over 11 years, after that I worked many years in a few day care centers.

In this time, we got married on June 30. 1976 after being engaged almost 2 years. Some people did not even think that we would be together more than a few months. It is now 47 years since I got engaged. We were together for 7 years, until 1981. I still lived in the same Apartment over 28 years with my animals. I lived there until 9/11. 2009, when I moved to where I still live today with my boy cat that was born in May 2002. My loving old man.

* *

In 2009 I wrote a short story for an RPG that I played online with friends. It played in outer space. I was able to choose my own figure, so that I took 2 figures that I liked and made them to my parents. I had all the abilities that they also had. It was fun to play with my friends, but 2010 we had to stop playing the game. I don't even remember why we had to stop playing.

....

I made a print of the story with my color printer so that I could always read the story anytime. Then years later in 2016, I had a dream that fitted into my RPG. After still remembering this dream over a week, I brought it on to paper. Then using my printer, I had the second part of this story. At this time the story was only for me so that everything was mixed up. It went from present, to past, then future, back to the past again. Back and forth like a ball, not making any sense to anyone but me. But at this time it did not matter anyway, the story was just for me.

Then around summer 2021, I told one of the social nurses that comes to me about the story. She said nice story, why don't you get it printed from a publishing company so that everybody can read it? I was not ready for this yet. I had a feeling the story was not yet finished. About this time, I had two more dreams that I brought to paper first. They had almost the same kind of background story.

So, I started asking around, where someone who had never written a book before can get something like this done? The owner of the bookstore where I always got my books told me where I could ask. So, I started working on the two stories with the same backgrounds. I put these two stories into one book together because of the backgrounds. But it took 3 versions of the stories and books to get them straight in German.

My bookstore lady told me if was not sure about my RPG names then just change them and the places too. By this time, I had a third dream around the RPG- Story. So, I also brought this dream to paper. That was when I started working on the RPG, it was in Winter 2021/2022. I started to rearrange the story many times, so it made some sense. It also 3 turns in German to get this book fixed. There is only one version out in English.

All of my Books are out in English & German. Written and translated by me.

My books in English are: first "Can Dreams Come True?- Or do you believe in Love at first Sight! There are two stories in one book with almost the same background. Second Résumé- Or The Story Of My Life.- And I's Just Playing Theater! 2 short stories in one book together. And last but not lease the RPG-Story. The Return of the Nehrus CBA-5142. The same books are also in German.

Well, how does Porky Pig from the Loony Toons say: " THAT'S ALL FOLKS!" It was Porky Pig who said this right? Or am I too old to remember this too.

I hope you enjoy reading this book and the others too as paperbacks' and as e-books on your Kindle Reader.

Yours truly, B. E. WASNER, In 2023.

* *

PS: I'm getting old, turning 70 years on March 30 this year (2023.) I have more Memories.

 It must have been New Years Eve 1969. We had friends over Visting to celebrate the day and we had a bowl of punch made from mineral water, sparkling wine and fruits like pineapples and strawberries.

Suddenly my little brother came into the room and was drunken, we asked him what he had done? He said: just eat some fruits. But the only fruits we had where in the punch, so everyone can think what had happened. Lilo just said: "show me what you ate."

Sometime later, I don't remember how long it was, our parents were not at home and my brother and I were fighting with plastic catsup bottles and spray cans of whipped cream. The red and white stuff was all over the walls, floor and even on the ceiling! Just all over the place, like when a bomb hits. I guess it was then too when I hit the old sink with my right wrist and broke it. I did not even know that it was broken. My doctor told me that years later by an x-ray exam of it.

When our parents got home, my brother and I got our asses whipped black and blue and we had to clean the kitchen too, from floor to the ceiling.

I quess that's all now. Bye......

THE END